STRONG

In the Running WITH

Ntando Mahlangu

by Kristy Stark

FAST READS

full tilt
PRESS

Ntando Mahlangu
TEEN STRONG

Full Tilt Press
42964 Osgood Road
Fremont, CA 94539
readfulltilt.com

Full Tilt Press publications may be purchased for educational, business, or sales promotional use.

Editorial Credits
Design and layout by Sara Radka
Edited by Renae Gilles
Copyedited by Nikki Ramsay

Image Credits
Flickr: US Air Force/Senior Airman Connor Estes, 21; Getty Images: Alex Livesey, 1, Alex Livesey, cover (main), Alexandre Loureiro, 3, Brian Bahr, 15, Bryn Lennon, 23, E+/ktaylorg, 19, E+/Obradovic, 20, iStock, 7, iStock, 17, Julian Finney, 16, Moment/ICHAUVEL, 26 (top), Victoria Marinyuk, cover (background); Newscom: AFLO/Kenjiro Matsuo, 14, Africaimagery.com/R de la Harpe, 6, EyePress/Tse Ka Yin, 9, Kyodo, 22, ZUMA Press/NurPhoot/Action Foto Sport, 18, 27 (bottom), ZUMA Press/NurPhoot/Kieran Galvin, 24, 27 (top), ZUMA Press/PA Wire/Adam Davy, 10, ZUMA Wire/Bildbyran/Johanna Lundberg, 4; Pixabay: tinabold, cover (accent); Shutterstock: Maria Moskvitsova, 26 (bottom), photastic, 29, Tashile, background; Wikimedia: Australian Paralympic Committee/Don Worley, 13, Organizing Committee of the Olympic and Paralympic Games Rio 2016, 11, Pierre-Selim, 8, Tasnimnews/Foad Ashtari, 12

ISBN: 978-1-62920-842-8 (library binding)
ISBN: 978-1-62920-854-1 (ePub)

CONTENTS

At 14 years old, Ntando Mahlangu smiled as he stood on a platform. The young man accepted a silver medal. He had placed second in the men's 200 meters. The race took place at the 2016 Paralympic Games in Rio de Janeiro, Brazil. The Paralympics is like the Olympics. But it is for athletes who have **disabilities**. Ntando runs on **prosthetic** legs. They are called running blades.

Ntando was one of the youngest people to race in the games. With his silver medal in 2016, he also set a new 200-meter record for Africa. His time was 23.77 seconds. This time was only 0.38 seconds behind the gold medal winner, Richard Whitehead. It was a huge achievement to win a medal. Ntando had only been walking for four years before he took home the silver.

disability: a physical or mental condition that damages or limits someone's abilities

prosthetic: an artificial body part that replaces a missing or injured body part

Getting Started

Mpumalanga is a province in northeastern South Africa. Most people in the province live in rural areas.

Ntando was born on January 26, 2002, in South Africa in the province of Mpumalanga. He was born with a medical condition called hemimelia. It kept his legs from fully developing below his knees. He did not have shins or feet. Because of this, he spent the first 10 years of his life in a wheelchair. In 2012, he made a decision. Ntando wanted to have both legs **amputated** at his knees. His parents did not want him to do it. But Ntando insisted. He wanted a chance to walk with prosthetics.

The surgery was not easy. It took time for Ntando to heal. Then he was connected with a **charity** called Jumping Kids. It is based in Pretoria, South Africa. That is the same city where Ntando now lives, trains, and goes to school. The charity helps children get prosthetics. Ntando told Jumping Kids that he hoped to play soccer with his friends and be their same height.

South Africa is known for its cultural diversity and natural beauty. It is home to about 57 million people, as well as many different kinds of plants and animals.

Jumping Kids was started in 2009 by Johan Snyders, who runs a prosthetics company. He realized that thousands of kids were living without access to prosthetics.

amputate: to surgically remove or cut off
charity: an organization that provides help and money for people in need

There are many adaptive sports, from archery and strength training to basketball and sailing. Athletes often try several before finding their niche.

Born to Run

Ntando said he felt like he started living once he received his running blades. He began to enjoy life. He could finally play soccer with his friends.

Ntando was asked about his favorite things to do since getting his blades. He gave an unexpected answer. He said that he liked being able to make tea for his grandmother. Before he was able to stand, he could not reach the table.

COACH CATHY LANDSBERG

Ntando trains with Coach Cathy Landsberg. The Jumping Kids Foundation introduced her to Ntando in 2015. Since then, they have worked together. Landsberg had a leg injury when she was 26. She fell off a horse. Her leg was amputated below her knee. After, she competed in **equestrian** events in the Paralympic Games. Now she coaches fellow **amputees**.

Before long, Ntando did more than play with friends. Running became his passion. And the young man had a talent for the sport. He quickly became an accomplished athlete. In 2015, he competed at the International Wheelchair and Amputee Sport (IWAS) Junior World Games. The event took place in the Netherlands. He credits that event with allowing him to compete at another level. He raced against athletes from all over the world. It was also the first time he traveled away from South Africa.

Equestrian events were first at the Paralympic Games in 1984. It has been featured at the games every year since 1996.

equestrian: related to horseback riding
amputee: someone who has had a limb surgically removed

Becoming Teen Strong

Ntando is much younger than veteran runners Richard Whitehead and David Henson. Whitehead said, "Mahlangu is really important. Hopefully I'm setting down a legacy for the next generation of athletes. When I retire, it's up to people like him to keep it afloat."

In July 2016, Ntando went to the IWAS Under-23 World Games. They were in Prague, Czech Republic. He won four gold medals at the competition. The runner set a new world record in the 400-meter race too. The IWAS named him Best Athlete of the Games for his performance.

Racing at the IWAS event helped Ntando. He became **eligible** for the 2016 Paralympic Games. Simply **qualifying** for the games was a huge achievement. Ntando never thought he would win a medal there. It was a thrill just to compete. He thought that anything else would be a nice bonus. His bonus came in the form of a silver medal—and having his amazing story shared with the world.

The 2016 Paralympic Games featured 22 different sports. Canoe and triathlon were added to the schedule, which already included athletics, cycling, and swimming, among many other events.

More than 4,350 athletes competed in the 2016 Paralympic Games. These athletes represented 160 countries around the world.

eligible: able to be chosen for or to participate in something because the right conditions have been met

qualify: to meet the conditions to be able to do something

Just like the Olympic Games, the Paralympics begin with an opening ceremony.

A New Sports Star

Ntando's performance at the games made people take notice. His name became widely known in South Africa. Many people were impressed by the young man's efforts. *Runner's World* called him South Africa's "New Paralympic Star."

Ntando received recognition from athletes and sports critics. He was awarded Newcomer of the Year in 2016. It is an outstanding honor given by South African Sports Awards. Ntando was grateful to everyone who supported him along the way. He said, "I just want to thank [South Africa] for allowing me to have this opportunity. Thanks to all the people back home who helped me get here."

The running world took notice of the teen, and he did not slow down. Ntando continued to compete and win races. At the 2017 World Para Athletics Junior Championships, he added another gold medal. He got a new world record for the T42–47 class in the 100-meter race. His time was 12.01 seconds. Ntando also broke the world record in the 400 meters. He did it in 49.92 seconds.

PARALYMPIC CLASSES

The Paralympics have groupings for the athletes. This keeps the games fair. For track athletes, there are 20 classes of **impairments**. Ntando's class is T61. This is for people who have a "lower limb/s competing with prosthesis affected by limb **deficiency** and leg length difference."

impairment: a condition that causes part of the body or mind not to work well

deficiency: a lack of something

Inspiring Others

At the 2016 Paralympic Games, Ntando came in first place in his heat, which is one round in a series of races. He then placed second in the final round.

Ntando is a confident person and a record-breaking athlete. He has overcome many challenges. This includes being in a wheelchair and learning to walk. That may have held others back. But this young man is not easily **intimidated**. Ntando believes in himself. And it shows, through the huge smile on his face.

In a short time, he has done what most athletes only dream of. Ntando has competed in many high-profile races. He has walked away with medals. But for the teen, competing is about more than simply winning. He also works with groups that help kids with disabilities, such as Jumping Kids. Since 2009, this group has worked to bring **mobility devices** to kids in South Africa. Jumping Kids is responsible for Ntando receiving his first prosthetics.

At the Paralympic Games, there are track-and-field events for men and women with visual, intellectual, and physical disabilities.

Richard Whitehead is a double amputee. He started running in 2003 at the age of 27. By 2020, Whitehead had a total of nine gold medals.

intimidated: to feel threatened or scared away from something

mobility device: something designed to help people with a disability move more easily, such as a wheelchair

Inspirations

Ntando inspires all athletes, not just Paralympians. The teen dreams about being an example to people. He wants them to chase their dreams as he has. Ntando uses social media to encourage others to believe in themselves and others. The athlete wants everyone to "know that no matter their situation, dreams are worth chasing and they can do it too."

The teen looks up to Paralympic athletes Samkelo Radebe and Arnu Fourie. They motivated him to qualify for the games. Both athletes

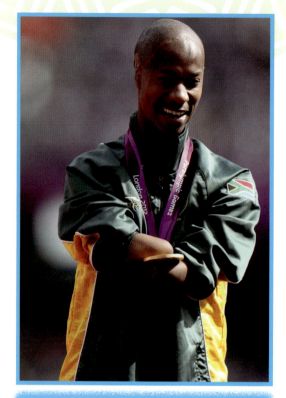

Ntando met Samkelo Radebe and got to hold his medal. "That was my motivation to try to get to Rio," Ntando said.

are from South Africa too. Unlike Ntando, these runners were not born disabled. They each suffered an accident that led to losing limbs. Radebe lost both his hands at age nine. Fourie had his left leg amputated after a boating accident. These runners won medals in the London Games in 2012. Ntando saw their achievements. They made him decide to train for Rio.

Now, through his own efforts, Ntando is inspiring others. "If I'm inspiring other people, then that means I am doing a good thing," he told BBC Sport Africa in 2018.

RUNNING BLADE

The running blade was invented in the 1970s. Since then, it has helped thousands of athletes compete. The cost of each running blade ranges from $5,000 to $40,000.

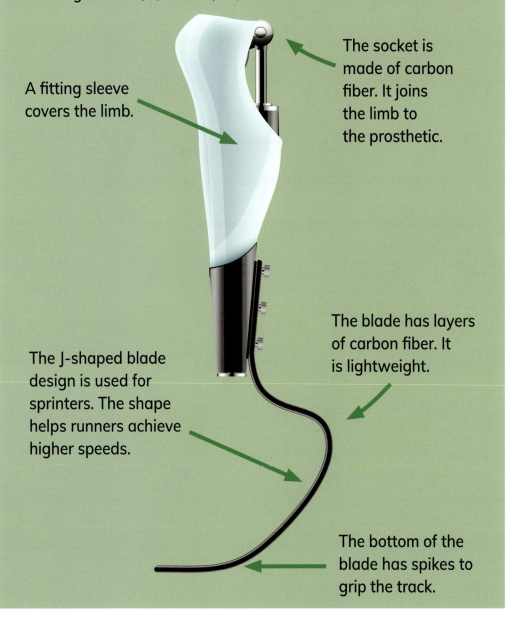

A fitting sleeve covers the limb.

The socket is made of carbon fiber. It joins the limb to the prosthetic.

The blade has layers of carbon fiber. It is lightweight.

The J-shaped blade design is used for sprinters. The shape helps runners achieve higher speeds.

The bottom of the blade has spikes to grip the track.

Work in Progress

In 2018, Ntando ran the 200 meters in 23.56 seconds in London. It was 0.21 seconds faster than his 2016 Paralympic medal race.

When he is not running, the teen works with many groups. In 2017, he became an **ambassador** for the Cartoon Network Africa. The TV channel has an anti-bullying campaign. It is called "Be a Buddy, Not a Bully!" The campaign brought attention to the issue of bullying. The network hoped to help children in Africa take a stand against bullying and **discrimination**.

On the network, Ntando shared his story. As a boy, he was bullied because he was different. Kids teased him when he was in a wheelchair. Because of his experiences, the teen was able to give kids advice about bullying and answer their questions. He credits talking with his family and friends for helping him get through those hard times.

About 6 percent of youths in the United States have a disability. These people are at higher risks for bullying.

ambassador: someone who represents a group while living in another country

discrimination: unfair treatment of a person or group of people based on being different or a minority

Bullying is a big problem. It is especially common in middle school. In the United States, 25 to 33 percent of students say they have been bullied at school.

People usually use different prosthetics for running and walking. As a kid, Ntando was only given blades because all he wanted to do was run.

Opportunities

In 2019, Ntando started a three-year partnership with Toyota. He is the face of their Start Your Impossible campaign. The campaign shows athletes who use mobility devices. It supports ways to make places more **inclusive** too. With Toyota, Ntando hosts athletic events for kids in South Africa. This partnership gives the teen chances to meet kids who have disabilities. His story can give them hope too.

Ntando was named a featured athlete for the Ossur company. It makes different types of prosthetics. In 2019, he represented Ossur in Iceland. Other Paralympians were there too. They celebrated the Life Without Limitations campaign. Ntando and the group even met the president of Iceland.

Also in 2019, Under Armour South Africa became Ntando's sponsor. This means that he appears in ads for the company. Under Armour gives him running clothes and pays for the cost of going to events. Sponsors often pay a **salary**, as well.

ATHLETE HANNAH McFADDEN

Hannah McFadden competed in her first Paralympic Games in 2012 at the age of 16. She was born with an irregular bone in her left leg and no left hip. The leg was amputated above the knee. Her classification is T54, which is for athletes with "full upper muscle power in the arms and some to full muscle power in the **trunk**. Athletes may have some function in the legs." In the 2016 Paralympic Games in Rio, she placed fourth in the 100-meter and seventh in the 400-meter races.

inclusive: not limited; open to everyone

salary: an amount of money that is paid to someone yearly

trunk: the center part of the human body, also called the torso

A Bright Future

Many new buildings are being built in Tokyo for the Paralympic and Olympic Games. The Ariake Arena is to host Paralympic wheelchair basketball, among other events.

Immediately after his win in Rio, Ntando began preparing for the Paralympic Games. Ntando qualified for the Paralympic Games in Tokyo with a win at the 2019 World Championships in Dubai. Ntando took the gold with a time of 23.23 seconds. Richard Whitehead came in second at 23.82 seconds.

After his 2019 win in Dubai, Ntando said, "To know that your past does not dictate your future is a powerful tool when it's matched with hard work and consistency. I am grateful for being able to perform and, in doing so, pave the way forward for those coming after me."

When he's not training, Ntando does things that most teens do. He goes to high school in Pretoria to finish his education. The teen hopes to study medicine or engineering at a university. Ntando has big dreams beyond training and running.

Erik Hightower, Noah Malone, Deja Young, and Jaleen Roberts represent the United States in para athletics events around the world.

Tokyo is the first city to host the Paralympic Games twice.

Ntando is carrying on a long tradition of representing South Africa at the Paralympic Games. The country earned its first medals at the 1964 games.

Not Afraid

Ntando has not let life's hardships get him down. He will not be slowed down either. The teen says that he was "born trapped" in his body. Because of this, Ntando says he is not afraid of pain or failure. Instead, the teen feels the constant need to move and keep moving after spending many years not being able to do so. Ntando pushes himself beyond what he ever thought was possible when he was in a wheelchair.

The young man has an important message to share with the world. He hopes to show others how to have **mutual** respect for the people around them. Ntando also thinks that anyone can inspire and influence people. He says, "You don't have to be the president to make a change in your country. You can just be a normal guy and you can make a change."

His extraordinary story, work ethic, and commitment to helping others certainly make Ntando Mahlangu Teen Strong.

mutual: shared between two people

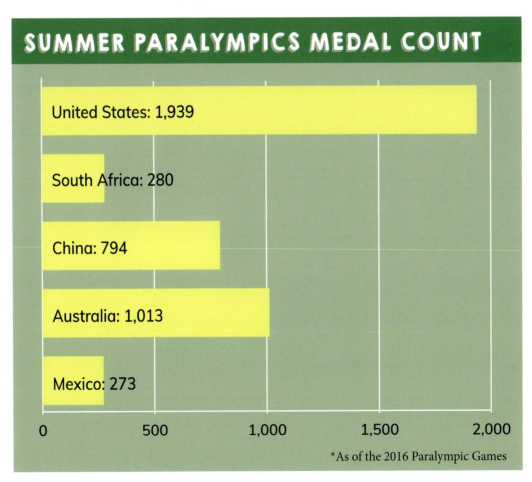

SUMMER PARALYMPICS MEDAL COUNT

United States: 1,939

South Africa: 280

China: 794

Australia: 1,013

Mexico: 273

0   500   1,000   1,500   2,000

*As of the 2016 Paralympic Games

Timeline

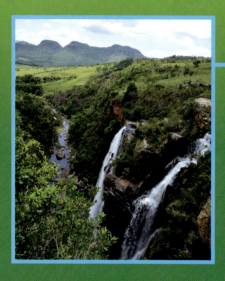

2002

Ntando Mahlangu is born in Mpumalanga, South Africa.

2012

At age 10, he has both legs amputated and is fitted for prosthetics.

2015

Ntando competes in his first international race and leaves South Africa for the first time in his life.

2016

At age 14, he wins the silver medal at the Paralympic Games in Rio.

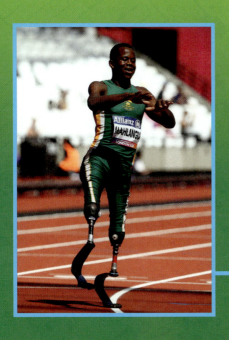

2016

Ntando is given the SA Sports Newcomer of the Year award.

2017

At age 15, he wins four gold medals and sets two world records at the World Para Athletics Junior Championships.

2018

Ntando beats Richard Whitehead and takes the gold medal at the Muller Anniversary Games.

2020

The teen focuses on one of the biggest races of his life: the 200-meter race at the Paralympic Games in Tokyo.

QUIZ

#1

In which event did Ntando take Paralympic silver in 2016?

#2

Ntando lost the gold medal to Richard Whitehead by how much time?

#3

What is on the very bottom of a running blade?

#4

How many classes are there for Paralympic track athletes?

#5

What does Ntando credit for helping him get through hard times?

#6

How many Paralympic medals does the United States have as of summer 2016?

1. The men's 200 meters
2. 0.38 of a second
3. Spikes to grip the track
4. 20
5. Talking with family and friends
6. 1,939

ACTIVITY

Ntando Mahlangu has overcome challenges and not let his disability stop him from achieving great things. What other teens with disabilities are also Teen Strong?

MATERIALS

- computer with internet access
- library access
- pencil and paper

STEPS

1. Research using the internet or library books to find one teen who has a physical or learning disability.

2. Find out how they overcame the disability. Research what they have accomplished in life despite the challenges they have faced.

3. Take notes as you find information.

4. Then create a presentation about the person to tell why he or she is Teen Strong. You can create a slide show, poem, report, or any other presentation.

GLOSSARY

ambassador: someone who represents a group while living in another country

amputate: to surgically remove or cut off

amputee: someone who has had a limb surgically removed

charity: an organization that provides help and money for people in need

deficiency: a lack of something

disability: a physical or mental condition that damages or limits someone's abilities

discrimination: unfair treatment of a person or group of people based on being different or a minority

eligible: able to be chosen for or to participate in something because the right conditions have been met

equestrian: related to horseback riding

impairment: a condition that causes part of the body or mind not to work well

inclusive: not limited; open to everyone

intimidated: to feel threatened or scared away from something

mobility device: something designed to help people with a disability move more easily, such as a wheelchair

mutual: shared between two people

prosthetic: an artificial body part that replaces a missing or injured body part

qualify: to meet the conditions to be able to do something

salary: an amount of money that is paid to someone yearly

trunk: the center part of the human body, also called the torso

READ MORE

Alexander, Lori. *A Sporting Chance: How Paralympics Founder Ludwig Guttmann Saved Lives with Sports.* Boston: Houghton Mifflin Harcourt, 2020.

Ganeri, Anita. *Journey Through: South Africa.* London: Franklin Watts, 2016.

Herman, Gail. *What Are the Paralympic Games?* New York: Penguin Workshop, 2020.

Long, Jessica Tatiana. *Unsinkable: From Russian Orphan to Paralympic Swimming World Champion.* Boston: Houghton Mifflin Harcourt, 2018.

Mayrock, Aija. *Survival Guide to Bullying: Written by a Teen.* New York: Scholastic Inc., 2015.

Osborne, M. K. *Track and Field.* Mankato, MN: Amicus Ink, 2020.

INTERNET SITES

http://beabuddy.cartoonnetwork.co.uk/
Get advice about how to handle bullies.

https://youtu.be/_CLKTwjWz-M
Watch a video of Ntando talking about his life.

https://www.teamusa.org/us-paralympics
Get the latest information about the Paralympic Games and its athletes.

https://youtu.be/8a5RRAACXI4
Watch a Paralympic basketball hopeful from Japan.

http://www.jumpingkids.org.za/about/
Learn more about the program that provided Ntando his first running blades.

INDEX